The Three Lucys

by HAYAN CHARARA • illustrated by SARA KAHN

LEE & LOW BOOKS INC. • NEW YORK

Text copyright © 2016 by Hayan Charara
Illustrations copyright © 2016 by Sara Kahn
LEE & LOW BOOKS Inc., 95 Madison Avenue, New York, NY 10016
leeandlow.com
Manufactured in China by Jade Productions, June 2016
Printed on paper from responsible sources
Book design by Christy Hale
Book production by The Kids at Our House
The text is set in Nofret
The illustrations are rendered in watercolor
10 9 8 7 6 5 4 3 2 1
First Edition

Library of Congress Cataloging-in-Publication Data
Charara, Hayan.
The three Lucys / by Hayan Charara ; illustrated by Sara Kahn. –First edition.
     pages cm
Summary: "A young Lebanese boy must learn to cope with loss and hope for
a peaceful future after losing one of his beloved cats because of The July War.
Based on the month-long conflict between Lebanon and Israel during
the summer of 2006. Includes Author's Note" –Provided by publisher.
ISBN 978-1-60060-998-5 (hardcover : alk. paper)
[1. Cats–Fiction. 2. Grief–Fiction. 3. Lebanon War, 2006–Fiction.] I. Kahn, Sara,
illustrator. II. Title.
PZ7.1.C49Th 2016
[Fic]–dc23   2015015906

For Lujaine, and all the boys and girls like him, and all the Lucys of the world—H.C.

For my dear husband, Steve Kahn—S.K.

On the hill behind our house in Lebanon, there is an olive tree. I like to sit in the shade of the tree with the three Lucys: Lucy the Fat, Lucy the Skinny, and Lucy Lucy. To the east there is a snow-peaked mountain. To the west is the salty sea where I learned to catch fish. North of where I live is a lush valley, and there is a lively city to the south.

People call these places by different names. Sometimes they fight about who owns the land. But the three Lucys don't care about names and who lives where. They only care about drinking milk, running after birds, leaping into my lap, and sleeping in the sun.

When I come home from school, I race up the steps to our house.

"Come, Lucy! *Ta'ala*, Lucy!" I call. I talk to the three Lucys in Arabic and English. I am learning both languages at school, so I am teaching the Lucys both languages too.

Lucy the Fat greets me with a big belly flop. Lucy the Skinny sits by my shoe and looks into my eyes. Lucy Lucy rubs her head against my legs and meows.

Sometimes when Mama and Baba aren't paying attention, I sneak the Lucys a treat. Lucy Lucy likes hummus. She licks it right off my fingertips. Lucy the Skinny's favorite treat is olives. She plays with them like toys. Lucy the Fat loves every kind of food!

Each summer Mama and Baba and I take a weekend trip to visit Mama's sister, Aunt Layla, and her husband, Uncle Adel. The Lucys stay at home. Before we leave, I fill their bowls with plenty of food and water and say good-bye to Lucy the Fat, Lucy the Skinny, and Lucy Lucy.

We drive to Beirut, the capital of Lebanon. Beirut is full of taxicabs, buses, and honking cars. Street vendors sell falafel sandwiches and freshly squeezed fruit drinks. The city is crowded with tourists, students, women buying groceries, parents pushing baby strollers, men thumbing prayer beads, and kids telling jokes and laughing on park benches.

When we arrive, Aunt Layla and Uncle Adel's house smells like warm bread fresh from the oven. There are books everywhere. It looks like Uncle Adel owns as many books as a library. He stacks them on shelves, on tables, on chairs, even on the floor.

In the mornings Mama and Baba look through the books, and Uncle Adel reads to me. In the late afternoons we go out to eat at a café and visit the waterfront. Sometimes there are musicians playing. At night we all climb the steps to the roof of the house to look at the stars above and the city lights below.

All weekend, Uncle Adel tells stories, and Aunt Layla keeps feeding us.

The weekend ends too soon. As we drive home from Beirut, I start to miss the city. I miss the waterfront and Aunt Layla's cooking and Uncle Adel's books and stories. But I'm excited to see the three Lucys again.

By the time we reach our town, the moon is high up in the sky. We drive past my school with its white-painted walls. I see the fig trees the teachers helped us plant last year. The road winds higher and higher up the hill toward our house. Below us the rest of the town is sleeping.

Then we hear a scream in the sky.

Baba stops the car. Mama peers out the window.

A red streak shoots across the horizon and a
loud boom fills the air. Then a fiery flash lights up the sky.

Baba quickly turns the car around and starts driving back the way we had
come, away from the loud crashes and bright flashes. He drives faster, faster, faster.

"What was that?" I ask. "Why did the sky turn red? Why aren't we going home?"

"It's not safe, Luli," Baba explains. "Those noises and flashes are from bombs."

My stomach sinks. Will bombs fall on our house, on my school, on our
neighbors and friends?

"Don't worry, Luli," Mama says. But I can tell from the look on her face,
something awful is happening.

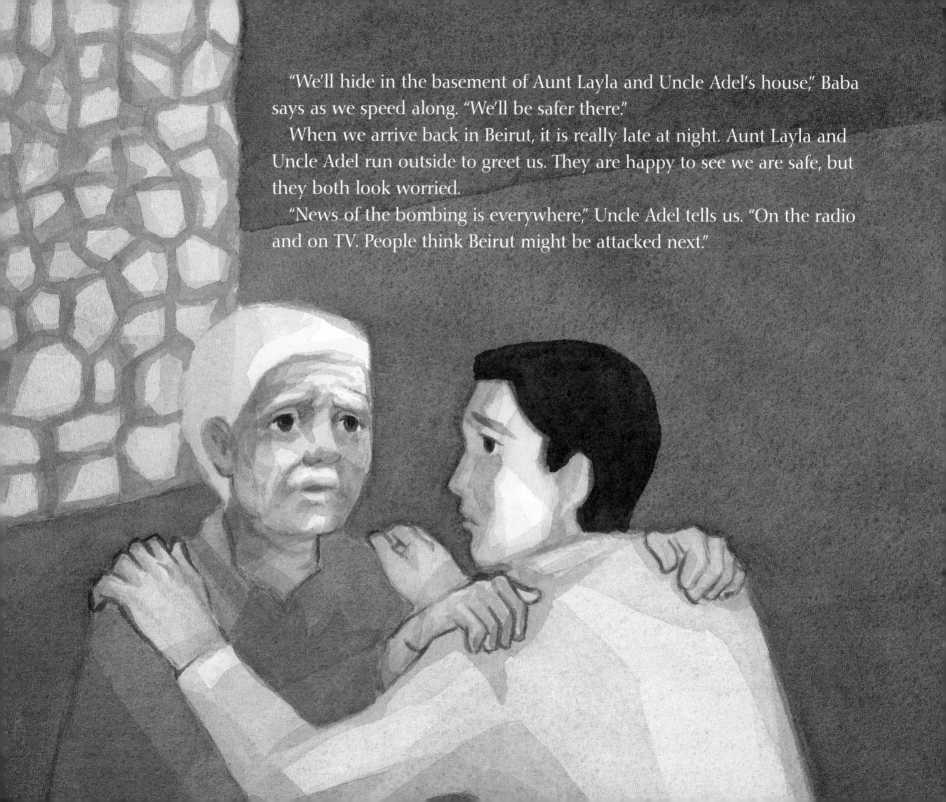

"We'll hide in the basement of Aunt Layla and Uncle Adel's house," Baba says as we speed along. "We'll be safer there."

When we arrive back in Beirut, it is really late at night. Aunt Layla and Uncle Adel run outside to greet us. They are happy to see we are safe, but they both look worried.

"News of the bombing is everywhere," Uncle Adel tells us. "On the radio and on TV. People think Beirut might be attacked next."

In the basement, we turn out the lights and sit together in the dark.
Uncle Adel tunes the radio to the news, but after a while Aunt Layla begs
him to turn it off. She's too upset to listen.

"It'll be okay," Mama keeps saying. "It'll be okay."

Baba and Uncle Adel move to a corner and start whispering to each other.
I wish I knew what they were saying.

After a while everything becomes quiet. No one talks. Even the crickets
outside stop chirping.

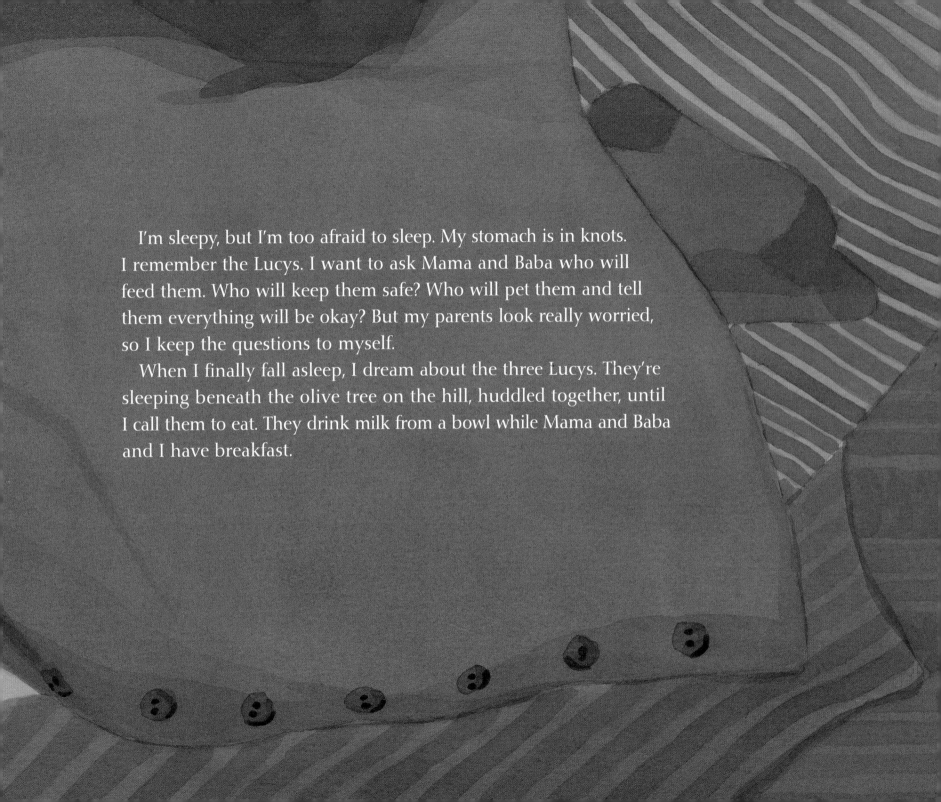

I'm sleepy, but I'm too afraid to sleep. My stomach is in knots.
I remember the Lucys. I want to ask Mama and Baba who will
feed them. Who will keep them safe? Who will pet them and tell
them everything will be okay? But my parents look really worried,
so I keep the questions to myself.

When I finally fall asleep, I dream about the three Lucys. They're
sleeping beneath the olive tree on the hill, huddled together, until
I call them to eat. They drink milk from a bowl while Mama and Baba
and I have breakfast.

The next morning, and every morning after that, Baba and Uncle Adel knock on the neighbors' doors to make sure they are all safe.

I borrow some of Uncle Adel's books. I like to look at the photographs and drawings, but I'd really rather be playing with the three Lucys.

In the afternoons the grown-ups sit around talking about who is to blame for the war. It's always the same. They start talking. Then they talk louder until they are shouting. Then they shout louder.

"Stop it," I yell one day. "You're worse than little kids!"

They look at me for a moment and then they all burst out laughing. It's good to hear everyone laugh again.

There is a calendar in Aunt Layla's kitchen with a big red X crossed through every day since the bombing started. Days turn into weeks, and the weeks turn into a month.

In the evenings, before the sun goes down, we head back to the basement. Sirens warn us about more bombs. The alarms sound like dogs howling. My heart pounds. I try not to be afraid, but I can't stop wondering where the bombs will fall next. And I can't stop thinking about the three Lucys at home. Are they okay?

On day thirty-four I'm playing a card game with Mama when Uncle Adel starts to shout.

"Cease-fire!" he yells. "There's a cease-fire!"

"What's a cease-fire?" I ask Mama.

"It means the fighting and bombing are over!" Mama says, and gives me a big hug. Everyone is smiling for the first time in weeks. Baba and Mama start to pack our bags. We're going home! Aunt Layla and Uncle Adel beg us to stay a while longer, but Baba wants to return home right away.

After Baba loads the car, we say good-bye. Aunt Layla and Uncle Adel tell us to drive home carefully.

As we drive along, the roads look like an earthquake opened them.
Bombs have fallen everywhere–on homes, restaurants, stores, and hospitals.
Now these places are just heaps of broken bricks, broken windows, and
broken doors.

In every town we pass there are people crying. Some are screaming.
Some are silent. They all look lost.

We pass my school and it is gone too. The bombings crumbled its white
walls, turning them gray and dusty. In the school garden, only one fig tree
is left standing. It looks lonely by itself.

We drive up the hill, and around another bend I see
our house. There are a few shattered windows and dust everywhere.
"Nothing that can't be fixed," Baba says, relieved. He stops the car.
I open the door and jump out. "Lucy! Lucy! Lucy!" I call.
Mama and Baba join in too. "*Ta'ala*, Lucy!" they shout.
We wait and wait and wait.

Finally we hear the tiniest noise: a meow. Out of a crawl space under the house, Lucy the Fat appears. She looks more like Lucy the Skinny now. I hold her tightly. She's frightened at first and tries to wriggle free. But once she recognizes me, she licks my face.

Then Lucy the Skinny peeks her head out. She meows over and over, as if she is saying, "Hello! Hello! *Marhaba!*" I lift her up and cuddle her in my arms. She is so skinny now, she weighs practically nothing.

I wait for Lucy Lucy to come out next. I wait a minute, two minutes, three minutes. I wait an hour. . . .

Each morning I call for Lucy Lucy. "Come, Lucy. *Ta'ala*, Lucy." Lucy the Fat answers and Lucy the Skinny answers, but Lucy Lucy never comes.

"Maybe Lucy Lucy is still hiding," I tell Baba. "Maybe she doesn't know the bombing is over."

Two weeks go by. One day I ask Mama, "Is Lucy Lucy ever coming back?"

Mama kneels beside me. "Luli, I don't think we will see Lucy Lucy again."

"Never?" I ask.

Mama takes a deep breath and nods.

My heart feels as heavy as an apple falling from a tree.

A few times a week I carry the two Lucys, one in each arm, to the olive tree on the hill behind our house. Lucy Lucy loved to sleep here. I look around. To the east the snow-peaked mountain is still there. To the west I still see the salty sea where I learned to catch fish. The valley is still to the north, and the city is still to the south.

Sometimes I walk to where my school was and watch the construction workers building new classrooms. Everyone works carefully around the only tree left in the school yard. Houses are also being rebuilt, and trees are being planted. Roads are being repaved. Little by little, our town is coming back to life.

At first when I thought of Lucy Lucy, all I could do was cry. But now I remember how much Lucy Lucy loved me, how she rubbed her head against my legs, how she greeted me with meows when I came home from school. Even when I'm sad, thinking of her also makes me happy.

Lucy Lucy is always in my memories and in my dreams, where there are no more bombings and the world is at peace. Lucy Lucy is safe, and she sleeps anywhere she wants.

Author's Note

The story of Luli and the three Lucys is based on true events. In the summer of 2006 war broke out on the border between Lebanon and Israel, an area with a long history of violence. On July 12, members of a Lebanese militia, Hezbollah, fired rockets into Israel. Three Israeli soldiers were killed and two others were captured. The Israeli armed forces responded with air strikes. Each day for just over a month, Israel launched between 3,000 and 6,000 bombs, rockets, and artillery rounds into Lebanon, devastating the country.

The short but destructive conflict is called the July War by the Lebanese. Parts of Lebanon, including the city where my family lived, were reduced to heaps of rubble. About 150 Israeli soldiers and citizens died, and the lives of more than 1,000 Lebanese were lost, most of them civilians. My grandfather was one of these civilians, as were a number of relatives and friends. Eventually a cease-fire was declared, and very slowly and painfully people began to rebuild their homes and their lives.

During this time, my little brother, whose nickname is Luli, was living in Lebanon. He was six years old, too young to have to experience the grief of war. This story is for him and for all the children of the world who, in the midst of larger conflicts, have lost people, places, and animals they love.